Do Cows Turn Colors In The Fall?

Library of Congress Cataloging-in-Publication Data

Woodworth, Viki.
Do cows turn colors in the fall? / Viki Woodworth.
p. cm
Summary: Simple, humorous rhymes ask a series of questions
about things that appear in the fall.
ISBN 1-56766-221-8 (hard cover : lib. bd.)
[1. Autumn—Fiction. 2. Stories in rhyme.]
1. Title.
PZ8.3.W893Doc 1996   95-44673
    [E]—dc20   CIP / AC

Do Cows Turn Colors In The Fall?

by Viki Woodworth

Viki Woodworth and family.

What turns many colors
in the fall every year?

A candycane?
A cow?
Leaves
or a deer?

(Leaves)

Who gathers food
for the winter to come?

(A chipmunk)

Who harvests crops
in the cool autumn air?

A farmer?
A fish?
A bone
or a hare?

(A farmer)

Who flies to the south
when winter comes?

A turtle?
A robin?

A train
or a drum?

(A robin)

Fall is the season
when animals scurry.

Winter is coming.
It's time to hurry.